Umbrella Weather

For Luke

Also by Hilda Offen in Happy Cat Books

Elephant Pie

Good Girl, Gracie Growler!

Happy Christmas, Rita!

HAPPY CAT BOOKS

Published by Happy Cat Books Ltd.,
Bradfield, Essex CO11 2UT, UK

First published 2001

Copyright © Hilda Offen, 2001
The moral right of the author/illustrator has been asserted
All rights reserved

A CIP catalogue record for this book is available from
the British Library

ISBN 1 903285 19 4 Paperback
ISBN 1 903285 20 8 Hardback

Printed in Hong Kong by Wing King Tong Co. Ltd

Umbrella Weather

Hilda Offen

Happy Cat Books

Here I am with my cat.
My cat's name is Bella.

We're off to the park
With my yellow umbrella.

'Brr! What if it snows?'
Bella shivers and shakes.

We have my umbrella!
We have magic cakes!

It can snow all it likes -
But don't worry, Bella.

We'll be cosy and warm
Underneath my umbrella.

'But what,' says my cat,
'If the snow turns to rain

And it thunders and lightnings
Again and again?'

I don't care! I'm not scared!
Let the thunder go 'Crash!'

I'll jump over puddles -
I'll 'Splish!' and I'll 'Splash!'

'But what if it's windy?
I'm bothered!' says Bella.

We'll be safe from the storm -
I've a yellow umbrella!

So let the wind blow!
Let it roar! I don't care

If we're whisked off our feet -
If we sail through the air.

We can run along rainbows
High up in the sky

And bounce on the clouds

As they go floating by.

'But what if we slip?'
Then we'll parachute, Bella.

'Will we land in the lake?'
Yes! But in my umbrella.

We sway on the waves -
The ducks start to laugh.

'Quack! Want to get back?
Just throw us your scarf.'

We're safe on the shore.
Three cheers, everyone!

Down comes my umbrella
And out comes the sun.